Angelina Loves . . .

Illustrations by Helen Craig Based on the text by Katharine Holabird

Grosset & Dunlap

Angelina Ballerina™ © 2006 Helen Craig Ltd. and Katharine Holabird. The Angelina Ballerina name and character and the dancing Angelina logo are trademarks of HIT Entertainment Ltd., Katharine Holabird, and Helen Craig. Reg. U.S. Pat. & Tm. Off. Used under license by Penguin Young Readers Group. All rights reserved. Published by Grosset & Dunlap, a division of Penguin Young Readers Group, 345 Hudson Street, New York, New York 10014. GROSSET & DUNLAP is a trademark of Penguin Group (USA) Inc. Manufactured in China.

Library of Congress Control Number: 2005016359

ISBN 0-448-44270-1   10 9 8 7 6 5

Angelina loves...dancing with her friends at Miss Lilly's Ballet School. Angelina dances everywhere! She loves spinning, twirling, and leaping.

Dancing makes Angelina very happy, but dancing isn't the *only* thing Angelina loves.

Angelina loves…her best friend, Alice. Angelina and Alice like to do all the same tricks, like hanging on the trapeze bar and cartwheeling round and round the playground.

Alice knows how to do some
things better than Angelina—
like perfect handstands.

But Angelina never stops trying, even if
she takes a tumble on the playground
and the other mouselings laugh.

Luckily, Alice is a good teacher.
She is patient with Angelina and
gives her lots of encouragement.

With Alice as her partner,
Angelina learns to do a
perfect handstand.

Angelina loves…the fair. But it's hard to do all of her favorite things when little cousin Henry comes along. Angelina loves soaring through the air on the Ferris wheel—but Henry hates the Ferris wheel.

Angelina loves zooming up and down the roller
coaster—but Henry hates zooming up and down.
Angelina loves the dark and twisty turns in the Haunted
House—but Henry hates anything dark and twisty.

Still, when Henry wanders
off without her, Angelina
gets very worried.

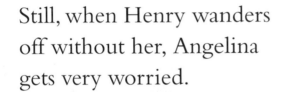

Then, when Angelina finds Henry again,
she remembers what she loves even more
than Ferris wheels and roller coasters.
She loves her little cousin Henry.

Angelina loves…riding bikes with Alice
down bumpy country roads.

When the road gets
a bit *too* bumpy…

…Angelina is especially glad to
have her good friend by her side.

Angelina loves…ice skating. Before the big
ice-skating show, Henry needs a little extra help.
Angelina and her friends let him hold their tails
so that he won't fall down on the slippery ice.

But how can they practice
when Spike and Sammy
keep bothering them?

Angelina learns that Sammy loves
doing funny tricks and that Spike
can skate backward…

... so she asks them to be in the show. She knows that if all her friends work together, the show will be better than ever!

Angelina loves…to work hard and to do her very best.
But things don't always go her way. When Angelina
gets sick before an important rehearsal, she's much
too dizzy to dance. Poor Angelina!

Angelina is very disappointed,
but when she feels better, she
decides to try again. And this
time, she dances beautifully.

Angelina loves…her family.

She loves the comfort of
her mother's arms when
she's feeling sick, or sad,
or even angry.

She loves the sound
of her father's fiddle.
When he plays for her,
she feels like a real ballerina.

And she loves dancing for
Grandma and Grandpa.
They are the very best
audience!

Angelina loves… her baby sister, Polly. Being a big sister isn't always easy. Polly gets lots of attention, and Angelina has to try very hard not to get jealous.

Polly tries to do everything that Angelina and her
friends can do, but she's too little. So Angelina
holds Polly and promises her that someday, she'll
teach her how to dance and do tricks, because…

... *that's* just what Angelina loves.